10 ten

9 nine

8 eight

7 seven

6 six

5 five

4 four

3 three

2 two

1 one

Ladybird books are widely available, but in case of difficulty may be ordered by post or telephone from:

Ladybird Books – Cash Sales Department Littlegate Road Paignton Devon TQ3 3BE
Telephone 01803 554761

A catalogue record for this book is available from the British Library

Published by Ladybird Books Ltd Loughborough Leicestershire UK
Ladybird Books Ltd is a subsidiary of the Penguin Group of companies
Illustrations © Trevor Dunton MCMXCVI
© LADYBIRD BOOKS LTD MCMXCVI
The author/artist have asserted their moral rights
LADYBIRD and the device of a Ladybird are trademarks of Ladybird Books Ltd

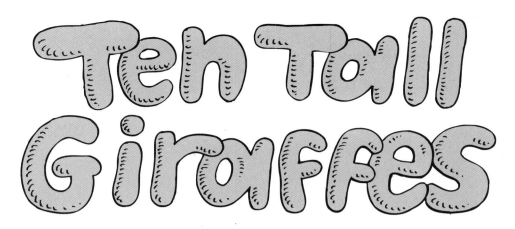

Ten Tall Giraffes

by Brian Moses
illustrated by Trevor Dunton

Picture
Ladybird

What's the hurry?
What's the fuss?
Why are all the animals
in such a rush?

10 ten

Ten tall giraffes...

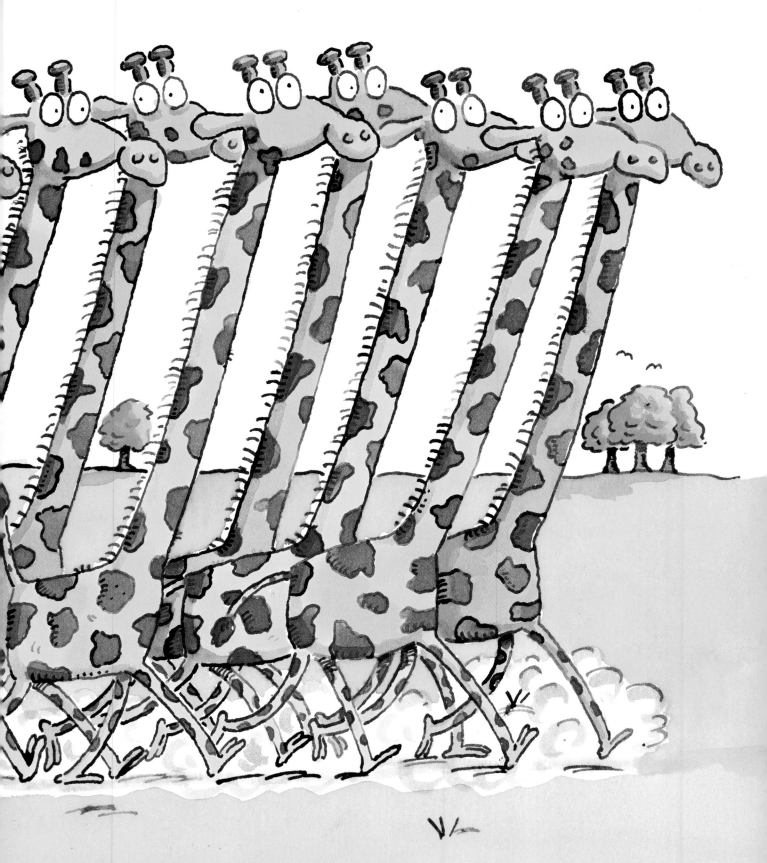

striding across the plain.

9 nine

Nine fierce tigers...

moving faster than a train.

8 eight

Eight massive whales...

racing through the sea.

7 seven

Seven silly monkeys…

swinging from tree to tree.

6 six

Six charging rhinos...

feet pounding on the ground.

5 five

Five angry bears...

making a terrible sound.

4 four

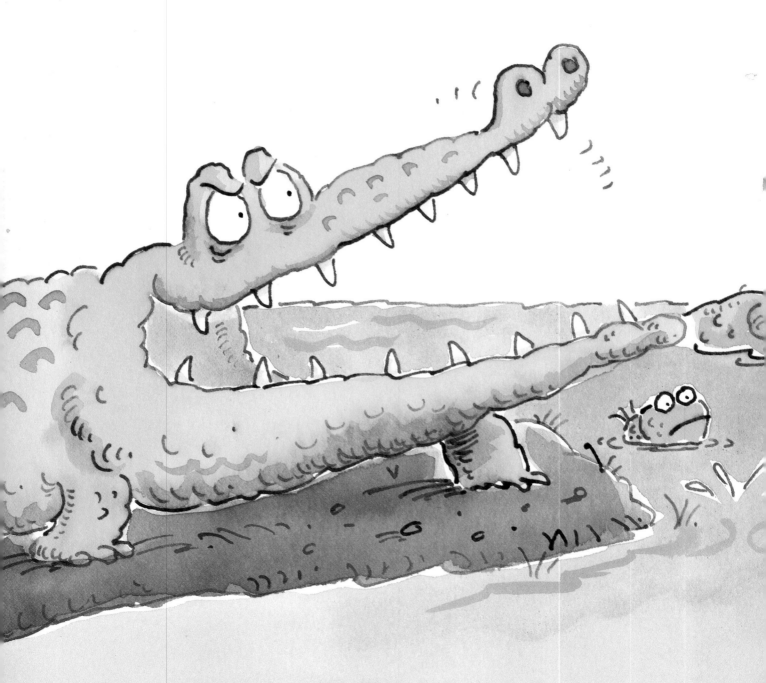

Four snapping crocodiles ...

don't get in their way!

3 three

Three excited elephants...

at the break of day.

2 two

Two jumping kangaroos ...

look how high they leap!

What's the special secret
that none of them can keep?

The ten... the nine...
the eight... the seven...

the six... the five... the four...
the three... the two...

1 one

It's one enormous party...

and you're invited, too!

10 ten

9 nine

8 eight

7 seven

6 six

5 five

4 four

3 three

2 two

1 one

Picture Ladybird

Books for reading aloud with 2 – 6 year olds

The exciting *Picture Ladybird* series includes a wide range
of animal stories, funny rhymes, and real life adventures that are
perfect to read aloud and share at storytime or bedtime.

A whole library of beautiful books for you to collect

RHYMING STORIES

Easy to follow and great for joining in!

Jasper's Jungle Journey, Val Biro
Shoo Fly, Shoo! Brian Moses
Ten Tall Giraffes, Brian Moses
In Comes the Tide, Valerie King
Toot! Learns to Fly,
Geraldine Taylor & Jill Harker
Who Am I? Judith Nicholls
Fly Eagle, Fly! Jan Pollard

IMAGINATIVE TALES

Mysterious and magical, or just a little shivery

The Star that Fell, Karen Hayles
Wishing Moon, Lesley Harker
Don't Worry William, Christine Morton
This Way Little Badger, Phil McMylor
The Giant Walks, Judith Nicholls
Kelly and the Mermaid, Karen King

FUNNY STORIES

Make storytime good fun!

Benedict Goes to the Beach, Chris Demarest
Bella and Gertie, Geraldine Taylor
Edward Goes Exploring, David Pace
Telephone Ted, Joan Stimson
Top Shelf Ted, Joan Stimson
Helpful Henry, Shen Roddie
What's Wrong with Bertie? Tony Bradman
Bears Can't Fly, Val Biro
Finnigan's Flap, Joan Stimson

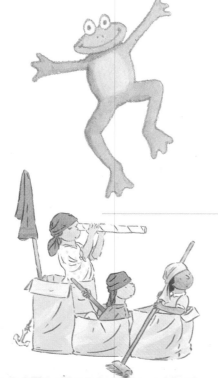

REAL LIFE ADVENTURE

Situations to explore and discover

Joe and the Farm Goose,
Geraldine Taylor & Jill Harker
Going to Playgroup,
Geraldine Taylor & Jill Harker
The Great Rabbit Race, Geraldine Taylor
Pushchair Polly, Tony Bradman

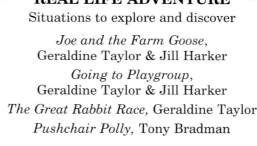